To a strong and mighty generation who will stay
the course firm and secure, as they remain anchored
to the truth and freedom found in Christ
—V. O.

LITTLE SIMON INSPIRATIONS
An imprint of Simon & Schuster Children's Publishing Division • 1230 Avenue of the Americas, New York, New York 10020
Copyright © 2009 by Victoria Osteen• Book design by Laura Reddick• All rights reserved, including the right of reproduction
in whole or in part in any form. • LITTLE SIMON INSPIRATIONS and associated colophon are trademarks of Simon &
Schuster, Inc. Manufactured in the United States of America • First Edition 2 4 6 8 10 9 7 5 3 1
ISBN-13: 978-1-4169-5550-4 • ISBN-10: 1-4169-5550-X

Victoria Osteen

Unexpected Treasures

illustrated by Diane Palmisciano

Little Simon Inspirations
New York   London   Toronto   Sydney

"Let's play pirates . . . I'm Captain Jon!
This pirate hat fits me.
So climb aboard my pirate ship.
We'll sail across the sea!"

"Ahoy! My name is First Mate Sue!
I see a ship in trouble!
That pirate ship has hit some rocks!
Let's sail there on the double!"

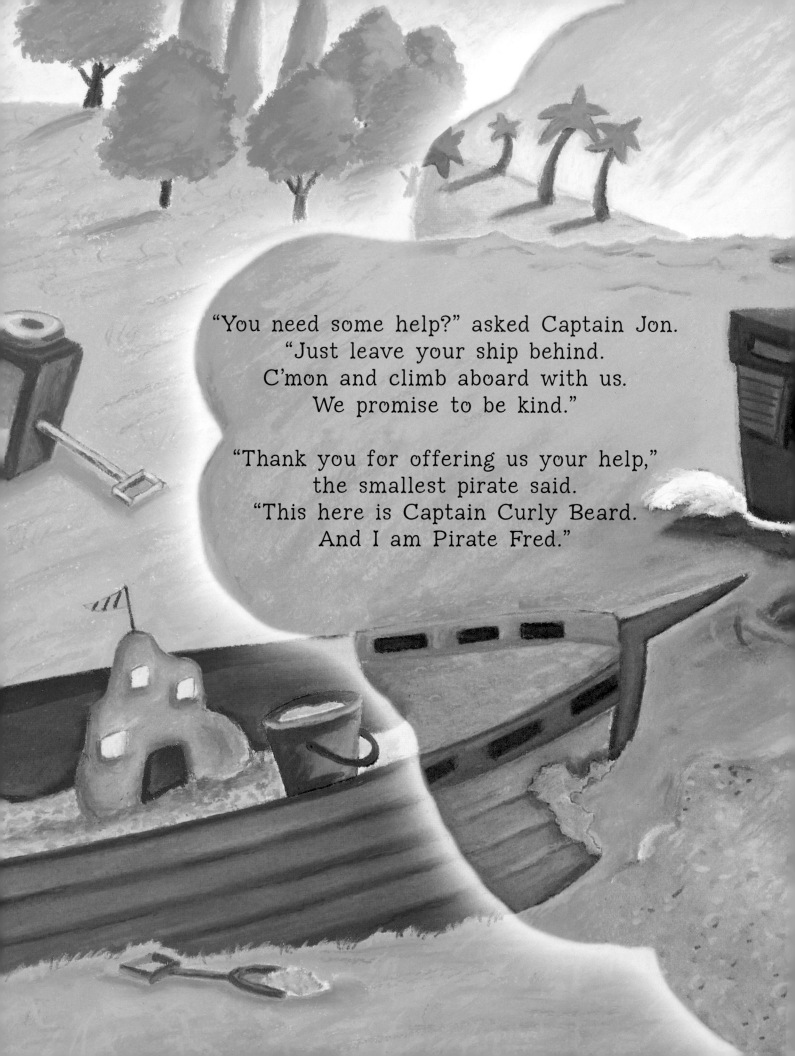

"You need some help?" asked Captain Jon.
"Just leave your ship behind.
C'mon and climb aboard with us.
We promise to be kind."

"Thank you for offering us your help,"
the smallest pirate said.
"This here is Captain Curly Beard.
And I am Pirate Fred."

"Oh, no!" cried Captain Curly Beard.
"There goes all of our treasure!
It's sinking fast. Our loss is great—
too great for us to measure . . ."

"Don't be too sad," said Captain Jon.
"It all will be okay.
Sometimes bad things can lead to good.
God always makes a way."

"We're sorry that you lost your gold,
but you found us," said Sue.
"You've made two lifelong friends today—
I'm one and Jon is too!"

"What good are friends without a ship?"
yelled Captain Curly Beard.
"It's your fault, Fred. You hit that rock!
If only *I* had steered . . ."

"I'm *sorry* Captain Curly Beard.
I tried my best," said Fred.
And then he pulled his pirate's hat
way down over his head.

"It was an accident," said First Mate Sue.
"We all make big mistakes.
Just keep on trying, Pirate Fred,
'cause you've got what it takes!"

"I suppose she's right," said Curly Beard.
"I'll try not to be mad.
I will not make Fred walk the plank.
I guess he's not so bad."

It's past my lunchtime, thought Curly Beard.
His stomach gave a growl.
Just then he saw a bowl of treats
and stole one with a scowl.

Then Captain Jon began to laugh,
"You ate a doggie treat!
You do not have to steal from us.
We'll *give* you food to eat."

"True friends treat others with respect.
True friends are kind," said Sue.
"True friends will share all that they can.
Let's feast like true friends do!"

"Thank you!" said Fred. "It all looks great!
"We're happy to attend!"
Curly hung his head in shame.
"I'd like to be your friend."

"You still seem sad," said First Mate Sue.
"Do you miss your boat?"
"I do," said Captain Curly Beard,
"but now our boat won't float."

"Please, take this necklace that I made—
they're friendship shells," said Sue.
"And when you wear it, don't forget!
It's love from me to you."

"Thank you," said Captain Curly Beard.
"Let's see . . . what have I got?
Let me give you my treasure map.
It's worth an awful lot."

"It's strange," said Captain Curly Beard.
And then he smiled real wide.
"This giving stuff is really fun.
I feel all warm inside."

"That's how it works," said Captain Jon.
"You feel good when you give.
So don't be greedy. Show your love!
That's how good pirates live."

"According to the treasure map,
we should be close," said Fred.
"But I don't see the treasure yet . . .
it could be up ahead!"

"Let's search some more," said First Mate Sue.
"That treasure is nearby.
Don't get discouraged, Pirate Fred.
Just hold your head up high!"

"Some things take work," said Captain Jon.
"And you might want to quit.
But don't give up! Success will come,
if you just stick with it!"

"That's right!" said Sue. "Success takes work.
But it's not far away.
Just keep believing! Don't give up!
You'll reach your goal someday!"

Then from the water up came Jon
swimming with a chest.
"Treasure!" yelled Captain Curly Beard.
"I never would have guessed!"

"We'll split this treasure," said Curly Beard.
"Here's ours, and here's your part."
"That's kind of you," said Captain Jon.
"You're giving from your heart."

"Today you have been doubly blessed,"
continued First Mate Sue.
"You have gold coins and gems and now . . .
you have a new heart, too!"

"This treasure is quite nice," said Sue.
"You've lots of precious gems.
But true peace and true happiness
are only found in Him."

"That's very true," said Captain Jon.
"God is the source of joy.
He loves us, and we love Him back.
He loves each girl and boy."

Then Pirate Fred dropped down his head—
"Does He love pirates, too?"
"Of course!" said Sue. "God loves us *all*—
and *all* means both of you!"

"Hey, there's your ship," said Captain John.
"At least it didn't sink."
"Whew! Just in time to change," said Fred,
" 'cause I am starting to stink!"

"Your ship can be repaired," said Jon,
"but there's a lot to do.
With teamwork we can fix the hole,
and make it sail like new!"

And so the friends worked really hard
until the hole was gone.
"Our ship looks great!" said Curly Beard.
"It won't sink now," said Jon.

"Thank you! Thank you!" said Pirate Fred.
"This means more than you know.
But now we must bid you farewell.
It's time for us to go."

"Just one more thing before you leave—
this is a gift," said Sue.
"Here is a special treasure map—
from both of us to you!"

"Oh, wow!" said Captain Curly Beard.
"I don't know what to say.
Your friendship is worth more than gold.
Now we must sail away."

"Remember! God loves you," said Jon.
"He'll help you do what's right.
He'll put good thoughts inside your heart.
They'll guide you day and night!"

"We call them Anchor Thoughts," said Sue.
"These thoughts will keep you strong.
They'll help you feel at peace inside—
even when stuff goes wrong."

"Thank you so much!" waved Curly Beard.
"We'll miss you lots!" said Fred.
And then they opened up the map
And this is what it said:

Nuggets of Gold Treasure Map . . .
the Journey Begins Today!

Trust the Lord with all your might!
He'll make your future super bright!

Become the best friend you can be!
You'll have more friends—just wait and see!

When you are kind in every way,
kindness returns. It knows its way.

When things look bad, don't lose your grin!
Just keep believing you will win!

Success is not that far away.
You're getting closer every day!

Your Anchor Thoughts keep you on course!
And they make you a mighty force!

Captain's Q & A

1. Captain Curly Beard and Pirate Fred discovered that friends can be a type of treasure. Name three friends that you consider "treasures in your life."

2. Captain Jon and First Mate Sue helped the pirates in this story without expecting anything in return. Why do you think it's important to help people?

3. Anchor thoughts helped Curly Beard and Pirate Fred learn to share with others. Can you think of times when you have shared good things with your friends?

4. Through God's love, Curly Beard became a better person. Can you think of things in your life that God can help you to do better?

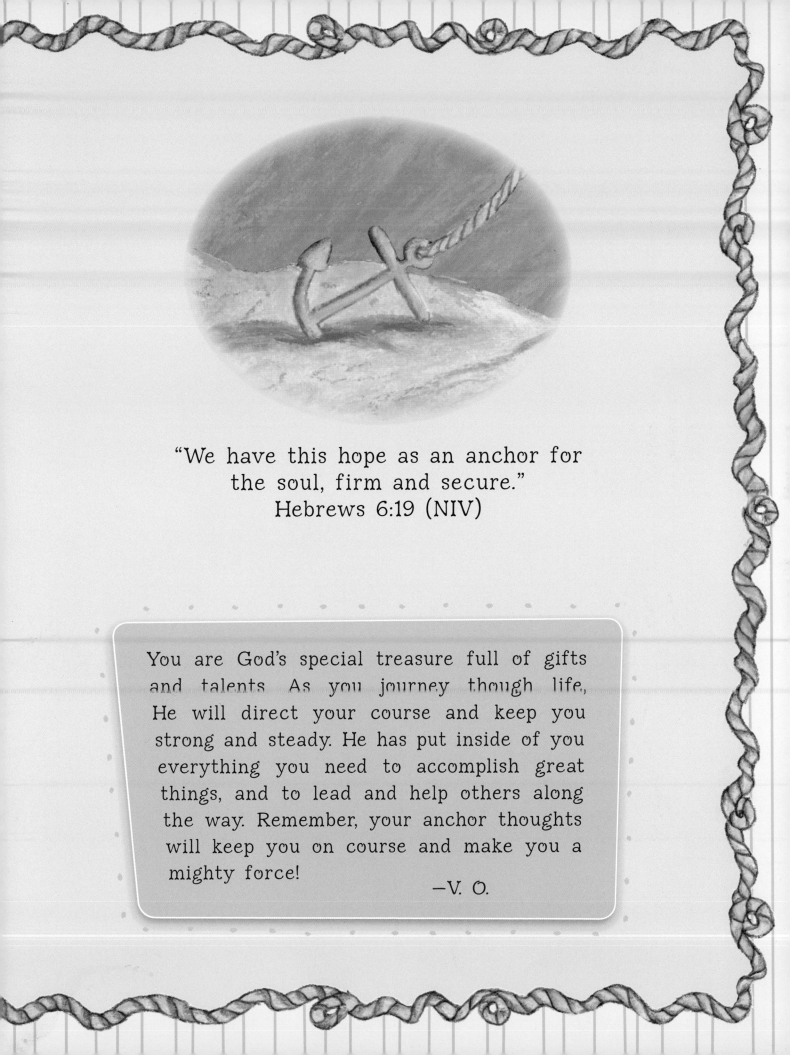

"We have this hope as an anchor for
the soul, firm and secure."
Hebrews 6:19 (NIV)

You are God's special treasure full of gifts
and talents. As you journey though life,
He will direct your course and keep you
strong and steady. He has put inside of you
everything you need to accomplish great
things, and to lead and help others along
the way. Remember, your anchor thoughts
will keep you on course and make you a
mighty force!

—V. O.